Elisha
the Eid
Fairy

Join the **Rainbow Magic Reading Challenge!**

Read the story and collect your fairy points to climb the

~~R~~ ... ~~he book.~~

D0248184

90710 000 464 202

ORCHARD BOOKS

First published in Great Britain in 2021 by The Watts Publishing Group

1 3 5 7 9 10 8 6 4 2

© 2021 Rainbow Magic Limited.
© 2021 HIT Entertainment Limited.
Illustrations © 2021 The Watts Publishing Group Limited.

HIT entertainment

A CIP catalogue record for this book is available from the British Library.

ISBN 978 1 40836 240 2

Printed and bound in Great Britain by Clays Ltd, Elcograf S.p.A

MIX
Paper from
responsible sources
FSC® C104740
www.fsc.org

The paper and board used in this book are made from wood from responsible sources

Orchard Books
An imprint of Hachette Children's Group
Part of The Watts Publishing Group Limited
Carmelite House, 50 Victoria Embankment, London EC4Y 0DZ

An Hachette UK Company
www.hachette.co.uk
www.hachettechildrens.co.uk

Elisha
the Eid
Fairy

By Daisy Meadows

ORCHARD

www.orchardseriesbooks.co.uk

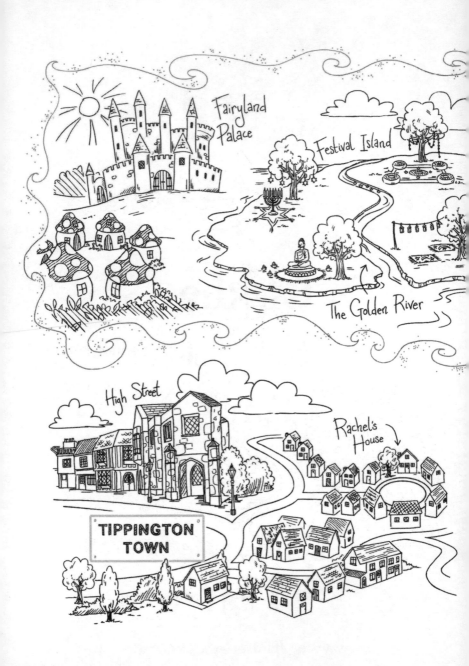

Jack Frost's Spell

Ignore Eid and Buddha Day.
Make Diwali go away.
Scrap Hanukkah and make them see –
They should be celebrating me!

I'll steal ideas and spoil their fun.
My Frost Day plans have just begun.
Bring gifts and sweets to celebrate
The many reasons I'm so great!

Contents

Chapter One
An Unexpected Visitor

The crescent moon was half hidden
behind wispy clouds, the midnight sky
glimmered with stars, and Rachel Walker
lay asleep in her bed. She was dreaming
of her many magical adventures in
Fairyland. Most people can only dream
of such a thing. But Rachel had often

visited Fairyland in real life. Only
her best friend, Kirsty Tate, shared the
wonderful secret that they were friends
with the fairies.

"Rachel!"

The loud whisper broke into Rachel's
dreams. Her eyelids flickered.

"Rachel!" came the whisper again.

Rachel frowned and opened her eyes.
It sounded like Kirsty. But how *could* it
be? Kirsty was miles away at home in
Wetherbury.

"I must have dreamt it," Rachel
murmured, closing her eyes and sinking
back into sleep.

"Rachel!"

The voice was louder, and this time
Rachel felt sure that she hadn't imagined
it. She sat up and stared around the

room. Who was speaking to her? She crossed her fingers. Please, *please* let this be the start of a new adventure!

"Hello?" she said.

There was an answering patter on the windowpane, like tiny drops of rain. Rachel jumped out of bed, her heart thudding with excitement. She ran to the window and flung open the curtains.

Moonlight spilled into the room, and Rachel gasped. Kirsty was outside, fairy-sized, fluttering her gauzy wings against the glass.

Rachel's fingers trembled eagerly as she turned the handle and opened the window. Kirsty slipped inside.

"Brrr, it's cold out there," Kirsty said, rubbing her arms. She was wearing pyjamas and a dressing gown. Rachel pinched herself to check that she wasn't still dreaming.

"How did you get here?" she asked.

"And why are you fairy-sized? What's happened?"

Kirsty flew to Rachel's bed and snuggled under the corner of her duvet.

"I was asleep until about ten minutes ago," she said. "Then I felt something tugging on my earlobe. It was Elisha the Eid Fairy."

"Of course," said Rachel breathlessly. "The new moon is in the sky. Eid starts tonight!"

Usually, the fairy adventures that Rachel and Kirsty shared lasted no more than a few days. But their most recent adventures had been very different. Jack Frost and his goblins had stolen the Festival Fairies' magical objects to create his own festival, Frost Day, and now festival days all through the year were in danger of being ruined. The girls had helped the fairies at Diwali and at Hanukkah, but there were two enchanted objects still to find.

"Elisha said that the Festival Fairies need to talk to us," said Kirsty. "She wanted us to come to Fairyland straight away. She turned me into a fairy and then waved her wand to bring us here to Tippington. But when the sparkles faded, Elisha wasn't with me. Rachel, she's vanished!"

Rachel darted towards her dressing table. She opened her jewellery box and took out the locket that Queen Titania had given her. Inside was a pinch of sparkling fairy dust.

"There should be just enough magic here to carry us to Fairyland," she said.

Rachel pulled on her dressing gown and then sat beside Kirsty and sprinkled the fairy dust over her own head. She felt a familiar tingle down her spine as she

shrank to fairy size. Pearly wings opened on her back, and she reached for Kirsty's hand.

"Please take us to the Festival Fairies," they said together.

Instantly, the room was filled with little specks of dazzling light that danced in the air like fireflies and clung to their hair and clothes. Soon, Rachel and Kirsty were shining from head to toe. Then the light grew even brighter, and Rachel's bedroom completely disappeared.

Chapter Two
Return to Festival Island

Rachel's legs wobbled as she and Kirsty landed on a white marble floor.

"I'm as dizzy as if I've been on a fairground ride," she said with a laugh. "Where are we?"

They looked around. A river was gleaming in the bright moonlight, and

they shared a happy smile.

"We've been here before," said Kirsty. "This is Festival Island, and that is the Golden River."

The last time they had visited Festival Island, it had been decorated for Diwali. This time, cut-outs of crescent moons dangled from the trees, and loops of green bunting were strung from branch to branch. There were balloons and purple lanterns, and flickering candles that spelled out the words 'Eid Mubarak'.

"I wonder what that means," said Rachel.

"It means 'Happy Eid,'" said a friendly voice.

Three of the Festival Fairies flew towards them from among the trees. Rachel and Kirsty hugged Deena the

Diwali Fairy, Hana the Hanukkah Fairy
and Bea the Buddha Day Fairy.

"Welcome back," said Deena. "We
really need your help. Where is Elisha?"

"We don't know," said Kirsty in an
anxious voice. "She vanished after she
magicked us to Rachel's house."

21

The fairies gasped and exchanged worried glances.

"Elisha wanted to invite our fairy friends to celebrate Eid here, even if she couldn't get her magical pelita lamp back from Jack Frost," said Bea. "But there won't *be* a celebration if we can't find her."

"Why did you want us to come?" asked Rachel.

"The goblins are back," said Hana. "They're causing trouble all over the island, and we need help to make them leave."

"What are they doing?" Kirsty asked.

"They're messing around with all the things that we use to celebrate our festivals," said Deena. "Lamps and lanterns, strings of bunting, balloons — they're all being spoiled by those naughty goblins."

"Deena and I have been able to cast spells to protect our decorations," said Hana. "But Bea's magic isn't working and Elisha is missing."

"If only I had my magical candle, I could have protected everything," said Bea with a sigh.

"Let's all go and find the goblins," said Kirsty. "Maybe we can work out a way to persuade them to leave."

The Festival Fairies led them through the decorated trees. They soon reached a small, beautiful clearing, circled by twined branches and climbing roses. It was decorated with more candles and lanterns, and golden crescent moons that twinkled in the moonlight.

"How beautiful," said Rachel.

"It's made from plants, trees and flowers," said Hana. "We love being surrounded by nature."

Nearby, loud voices were squawking and squabbling. Smashes and crashes echoed around the little glade and then five goblins rampaged into the clearing. Flowers and candles were trampled under their feet, and the crescent moons were torn from the branches.

"Please stop!" cried Kirsty.

The goblins whirled around at the sound of her voice. A few of them blew raspberries. But the tallest of them took a step towards the fairies, smirking.

"Made you look, made you stare," he jeered. "Now Jack Frost has got the Eid Fairy."

"*That's* why the goblins came back,"

said Rachel. "They caused trouble here to make her travel to the human world to ask for help. Then Jack Frost kidnapped Elisha."

"And now he's going to make her tell him how to use the Festival Fairy magic," said the goblin in a boastful voice.

There was a loud crackle, and five lightning bolts flashed to the goblins' feet. The goblins jumped on to them as if they were surfboards and whizzed away from the clearing, wobbling wildly.

Bea stared around at the mess.

"Poor Elisha," she said. "Oh my goodness, I hope we can put things right. Celebrations must be going wrong all over the world. I'm worried that our Festival Fairy magic might not be strong enough to repair everything while two of our magical objects are still missing."

"We have to find Elisha and the pelita lamp," said Kirsty. "There's no time to lose."

"But it's going to take all our magic to repair the mess the goblins have made," said Deena. "We have to stay here."

Rachel and Kirsty shared a determined smile.

"That's OK," said Kirsty. "Rachel and I will rescue Elisha."

"Yes, we'll fly to the Ice Castle while you're putting things right here," said Rachel.

Hana, Deena and Bea put their arms around Rachel and Kirsty.

"If anyone can free Elisha, it's you two," said Hana, smiling at them. "Good luck!"

Chapter Three
Ice Prison

Rachel and Kirsty whooshed into
the sky. The sea was sparkling in the
moonlight, and mermaid tails flicked out
of the water.

"I wish we could say hello," said Kirsty
as they zoomed towards the Ice Castle.

But there was no time to stop. They

were on a mission to rescue their friend
and save Eid. Soon, the grim, cold walls
of Jack Frost's castle rose up ahead of
them.

"Something is shining on top of the
castle," said Rachel, feeling confused.
"What could it be?"

There were more than twenty tiny
sparkles on the battlements.

"They look like far-off fairy lights,"
said Kirsty. "But they can't be. Jack
Frost wouldn't decorate his home with
anything so pretty."

They were closer now, and they could
see the silhouettes of goblins on the castle
walls. The sparkles were coming from
their eyes.

"Oh my goodness," cried Rachel.
"They're binoculars, not fairy lights –

and they're all pointing at us!"

The goblins started to yell and jump up and down. Rachel and Kirsty paused and hovered in the air. The goblins stepped back, and made way for a tall, spiky silhouette.

"I can't see his face," said Kirsty. "But that's Jack Frost, and he knows we're here."

"We can't go back without Elisha," said Rachel. "We have to help her."

"My heart is fluttering as fast as my wings," said Kirsty.

Slowly, they flew closer to the Ice Lord. Now they could see his sharp nose and his cruel mouth. Rachel felt her best friend shiver.

"I knew you pesky fairies would come here," said Jack Frost, curling

his thin lips into a sneer. "I ordered the goblins to look out for you. Turn around and go home!"

His breath hung like mist in the air, then froze into icy drops that tinkled to the ground.

"Not without Elisha and the pelita lamp," Rachel called out, trying to sound brave.

"That lamp is mine," Jack Frost snarled, folding his arms. "I just have to make it obey me. Then I'll turn Frost Day into the only festival worth celebrating. I'll have a feast of amazing food and make all the fairies jealous."

"Please think about other people," said Kirsty, clasping her hands together. "This is such a special time for Muslims everywhere. People will be exchanging

presents, lighting lamps and spending
time with their families and friends.
Please don't spoil it."

Jack Frost lifted one arm and pointed a
bony finger straight at them.

"I don't care about Eid or any of
your other silly festivals," he hissed. "I
told those pesky fairies to make me a
festival, and they should have obeyed me.
Whatever happens is all their fault."

The goblins squawked with laughter.

"That told you!"

"Clear off, you flappy little fairies."

"Where is Elisha?" Rachel asked.

Jack Frost gave a mean laugh.

"Let's just say that her magic has been
put on ice," he said. "She's my prisoner
until she tells me how to work the pelita
lamp. And now it's time for you to go."

He flicked his wand, and there was
a flash of blue lightning. *WHUMP!*
Something flung Rachel and Kirsty
sideways.

"Oh help!" cried Kirsty as they tumbled
head over heels away from the castle.

"I can't stop!" Rachel squealed.

They spun and whirled through the

cold night air. It seemed like hours before they slowed down and reached for each other.

"I hardly know which way is up," said Kirsty with a groan.

The best friends hovered weakly in the air.

"Oh my goodness," said Rachel. "I'm glad that my wings are still working. My legs feel like jelly."

"Where are we?" asked Kirsty. "My head is still spinning."

Rachel looked down and saw flickering lights inside a crowd of little huts below. A few thin spirals of smoke were rising up from the huts.

"I think we're above Goblin Grotto," she said. "It's strange to think of all the goblins inside their homes, with no idea

that we are above them."

Kirsty stared into the distance and gasped.

"Look at the Ice Castle," she said in an amazed voice.

A thin, white tower was shining in the moonlight, at the side of the castle.

"Why didn't we see it before?" asked Rachel.

"We couldn't see it from the front," said Kirsty. "But from here, it's easy to spot."

"There's something whirling around it," said Rachel. "It looks like a storm, but how could it be? It's not even snowing."

They rose higher to peer at the strange

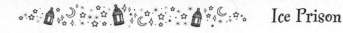

tower. A wind was whooshing around it, making the tower look blurry.

"There's something glittering inside that wind," said Rachel.

"I think it's hail," said Kirsty, feeling confused. "But why would Jack Frost build a new tower and attack it with a hailstorm?"

Jack Frost's words popped into Rachel's mind. "*Her magic has been put on ice.*" And suddenly, she knew why Jack Frost had built the tower.

"Oh, Kirsty, Jack Frost meant exactly what he said," she cried. "Elisha is trapped in the ice tower!"

Chapter Four
The Wand Hunt

"We have to go back," said Kirsty. "I hope that the goblins have put their binoculars away."

They flew slowly and low, keeping their eyes on the battlements. Would a goblin peer over the top and spot them? The closer they got, the stronger the icy blast

from the hailstorm became. The wind
whistled as it hurtled around the tower.

"Brrr," said Rachel. "I wish we were
wearing something warmer than dressing
gowns."

They were so close to the tower that
the hailstones were peppering their faces.
They stopped and tried to see through
the swirl of snow and ice.

"It's just a smooth tower," said Kirsty. "I
don't think there's a way in."

There was no door at the bottom.
Rachel and Kirsty flew upwards, looking
for windows, but there didn't seem to be
a single one. They had almost given up,
when the wind grew calmer for a few
seconds. In that moment, Kirsty spotted
something.

"Look!" she exclaimed.

At the very top of the tower was
a single, small window. Through the
whirling hail, they glimpsed a figure
sitting at the window. She was wearing a
pink hijab with jeans and a white shirt.
Her arms were wrapped tightly around
her knees.

"Elisha!" they
called together.

The little
fairy heard
them and
jumped to her
feet.

"Rachel!
Kirsty!" she
cried. "Oh,
thank goodness.
Jack Frost

locked me in here and I can't get out."

"We know," Rachel shouted to her over the howling wind. "He wants you to show him how to use the pelita lamp."

"I'll never help him to spoil Eid," said Elisha in a loud, determined voice. "He'll have to keep me locked up for ever."

"We won't let that happen," said Kirsty. "We're here to rescue you."

She shared a worried look with her best friend. How were they going to set Elisha free? They couldn't even get close to the tower.

"The window is too small to climb through, even if we could get past the hailstorm," said Kirsty.

"Do you have your wand?" Rachel asked.

Elisha shook her head.

"Jack Frost took it from me when he made the tower," she said, her head drooping. "He dropped it into the deep snow below and laughed when it sank. Without my wand, I'm helpless."

"We'll find it," said Kirsty in a determined voice.

She and Rachel dropped down to the thick snow that was heaped up around the tower.

"Let's start digging," said Rachel, rolling up her dressing gown sleeves. "This is going to be cold work!"

They plunged their hands into the snow and gasped at the cold.

"My fingers are numb already," said Kirsty. "I feel as if it's freezing my bones."

"We have to keep going," said Rachel.

They were both soon covered in a thin layer of frost. Their arm hairs crackled stiffly, and their eyelashes turned white.

"Keep moving your wings," said Kirsty, shivering. "If they freeze, we won't be able to fly."

"Even m–my t–teeth are c–cold," said Rachel, her teeth chattering.

Over and over again, they pushed their hands into the snow and stretched out their fingers. Over and over again, they felt nothing but snow in their hands.

"I feel as if Jack Frost is laughing at us," said Rachel.

"Come on, wand," Kirsty whispered. "You must be here somewhere."

Suddenly, Rachel's fingertips brushed

against something. Her hands were so numb that it was difficult to hold on to anything, but she squeezed as hard as she could and gave a mighty tug. There was an explosion of snow, and Rachel fell backwards, clutching a delicate wand.

"We've got it!" she cried out. "Elisha, we found it!"

Shuddering with cold, Rachel and Kirsty zoomed up to the tiny window at the top of the tower. Elisha gave a twirl of happiness when she saw them.

"I can't believe you've found it," she called out. "But how can you get it to me?"

The hailstorm was raging around the tower.

"We'll be whooshed away in a second if we try to fly through that," said Rachel.

"The wind dropped for a moment earlier on," said Kirsty. "Maybe it will do that again."

Hardly daring to breathe, the fairies waited. Eid celebrations all over the

world depended on Elisha getting her
wand back. After a few moments, the
howling grew quieter and the swirling
wind slowed down.

"It's now or never," said Rachel to herself.

She aimed the wand at the little window, her heart pounding.

"I know you can do it," said Kirsty.

Hoping Kirsty was right, Rachel took a deep breath . . . and threw the wand.

Chapter Five
The Feasting Table

"Got it!" cried Elisha.

She waved her wand above her head in triumph. A purple light spilled from the tip and flooded the tower.

"The ice is melting," Rachel exclaimed.

Kirsty cheered and hugged her best friend. As they watched, the wind faded away and the walls of the tower melted from the top down. Water tumbled to the ground, where it froze again in the middle of a mighty splash. Elisha zoomed towards Rachel and Kirsty and wrapped her arms around them.

"Thank you for coming to get me," she said warmly. "I would still be a prisoner without you."

A purple bubble surrounded them, and they felt warmth slipping around their shoulders like a cosy blanket.

"I've cast a spell to keep us warm while we're here," said Elisha.

"That's good," said Kirsty. "Because I think we have to go inside the castle."

The three fairies looked at each other. It was a bit scary to think of going into the castle to get the pelita lamp. If they were caught, Jack Frost might lock them all in a tower.

"We have to save Eid feasts around the human world," said Elisha.

The fairies linked arms and flew closer to the castle.

"Elisha, what does the pelita lamp do?" Rachel asked.

"It helps me make sure that Eid is a happy, special time for Muslims," said Elisha. "You see, tonight is the end of Ramadan."

"I've heard about Ramadan," said Kirsty. "It's a month when Muslims don't eat or drink between dawn and sunset, right?"

"That's right," said Elisha. "It ends when the new moon appears – and that's tonight. Then we celebrate with a feast."

They reached the battlements and peeped over the top. There were lots of binoculars scattered around, but no goblins.

"What happens at the Eid feast?" asked Rachel.

"It's so much fun," said Elisha, her face lighting up. "We fill plates and pots to the brim with sweet, yummy food, and we give to charity, and offer gifts to the people we love."

The fairies fluttered over the top and landed on the battlements.

"It sounds like a really happy celebration," said Kirsty.

"It's a time of love, forgiveness and thankfulness," Elisha went on, looking around. "And hugging. Lots and lots of hugging! It's hopeful, and fun, and the

exact opposite of everything Jack Frost
stands for. But where is he? And where
are all the goblins?"

The fairies looked around. There was
no one on the battlements or in the
courtyard below. There were no cackles,
squawks or sounds of running feet.

"Where have they gone?" asked Elisha.

Kirsty whirled around and flew to look
down at the gardens behind the castle.
The blue-and-silver festival tent they had
seen during their adventure with Deena
had disappeared. In its place was a huge
feasting table, draped with a blue-and-
silver tablecloth and decorated with
lightning bolts.

"Let's get closer," said Rachel.

They swooped down and saw plates
filled with Turkish delight, baklava and

dates. There were biscuits that smelled so good their mouths watered.

"Those are *kleichas*," said Elisha. "They're rose-flavoured with nuts and dates inside. Oh yum, look – there's honey cake too."

Then she gasped and fluttered backwards. Rachel and Kirsty pulled her down to hide behind a frozen bush. Two goblins were pacing up and down beside the table. They were wearing tall chef's hats and grubby aprons.

"We have to stop the lamp making Eid food," said the first goblin, his hands on his hips.

"But how?" wailed the second goblin. "I don't know how the lamp magic works.

Every time I ask it to make a Frost Day feast, it makes this stuff. How are we supposed to teach the silly thing to make bogmallows?"

He lifted his chef's hat, and the fairies had to stop themselves from shouting out in excitement. Under his hat was a beautiful purple lamp. Its soft light spilled out across the feasting table.

"That's it," whispered Elisha. "My pelita lamp!"

The first goblin started chewing his nails in worry.

"You're probably just teaching it wrong," he said with a sneer. "Jack Frost is going to be furious, and I'll tell him it's all your fault."

"I tried to teach it to make iced thunder burgers," said the second goblin, putting his hat back over the lamp. "It just keeps making those silly pitta breads. Yuck!"

"If Jack Frost can't have iced thunder burgers on Frost Day, we're in big trouble," said the first goblin.

"And here he comes," whispered Kirsty.

At the far end of the garden, Jack Frost was striding along in a crowd of goblins. They were lit up by blue lanterns, and they were heading straight towards the feasting table.

"He's coming to check up on us," wailed the second goblin.

"We have to get the lamp back before Jack Frost arrives," said Rachel in an urgent voice. "What are we going to do?"

Chapter Six
A Dizzy Dance

"Perhaps I could swoop over their heads and take the pelita," said Elisha in a low voice.

"The goblin would grab you before you could fly away," said Rachel. "They're super quick. It's too risky."

"What if the goblins were dizzy?"

Kirsty suggested. "They would be too wobbly to stop us."

"But how can we make them dizzy?" Elisha asked.

Kirsty crossed her fingers.

"I've got an idea," she said. "I just hope it works. Elisha, can you turn Rachel and me into dance teachers?"

Elisha looked puzzled, but there was no time to ask questions. Jack Frost was getting closer. She waved her wand, and their dressing gowns and wings vanished. Each of them was wearing a leotard, a long black skirt and a pair of high-heeled shoes.

"You don't look like you," said Rachel, rubbing her eyes. "It's as if I can't quite see your face. Every time I try to look at you, it's just a blur."

"Same here," said Kirsty.

"It's a special spell," said Elisha, smiling. "But it won't last long. Hurry!"

Rachel and Kirsty darted out into the moonlight. The first goblin let out a squeal of surprise.

"Who are you?" he cried.

"We're here to teach you how to dance," Kirsty exclaimed. "It's a new part of the Frost Day plans. Everyone has to learn it!"

Without giving the goblin time to
think, she whirled him into a dance,
spinning, hopping and skipping around
the feasting table.

"You too," said Rachel, taking the
second goblin's hands.

"But I don't like dancing," the goblin
wailed. "My feet aren't made for it. It
makes me feel sick."

"Shut up," the first goblin snapped, panting. "If Jack Frost says we have to learn a dance, then that's what we have to do."

"Goody two shoes," the second goblin yelled.

Round and round they danced, faster and faster. The goblins kept shouting insults at each other, and Jack Frost was getting closer and closer. Kirsty glanced at Rachel and saw that her black outfit was turning into a soft, fluffy dressing gown. The spell was fading.

"Final twirl!" Kirsty exclaimed. "Big finish!"

She and Rachel sent the goblins into one last, huge twirl and let them go. They whizzed around the table like two large, green spinning tops, and Elisha zoomed out from behind the bush. She plucked the hat from the second goblin's head, lifted the lamp and replaced the hat. The goblin didn't even notice.

"Hide!" she cried out.

Panting and dizzy, Rachel and Kirsty flung themselves back behind the bush with Elisha. The spell had worn off, and they were fairies again. At the same moment, Jack Frost strode around the corner. The spinning goblins crashed into him, and they all fell down like skittles.

"You idiots!" Jack Frost yelled. "Nincompoops! Mushroom heads!"

Stifling their laughter, the fairies shared a happy hug. The pelita lamp glowed in Elisha's hands.

"It's beautiful," said Rachel, running her finger over the delicate carvings.

"And it's back where it belongs, thanks to you two," said Elisha. "How can I ever thank you?"

"Knowing that Eid will be a happy festival is all the thanks we need," said Kirsty, smiling at her. "Now there is only one magical object left to find."

At that moment, Jack Frost let out a yell of rage.

"What do you mean, it's *gone*?"

"I think it's time for us to leave," said Elisha. "I must return to Festival Island, and you need to get back to your beds.

Eid Mubarak, Rachel and Kirsty."

"Eid Mubarak to you too," they replied.

Elisha waved her wand above them, and they were sprinkled with fairy dust. Some went into their magical lockets, and some landed on their eyelids. They both started to yawn.

"Oh my goodness, I'm so sleepy all of a sudden," said Rachel.

She snuggled deeper into her dressing gown and closed her eyes. Her head rested on something soft

and cosy. Rachel forced her tired eyes to flicker open, and gasped. She was lying in her own bed in Tippington, and she was a human again. The crescent moon was shining in through her open curtains.

Rachel smiled and let her eyes close. She knew that a few miles away in Wetherbury, her best friend was doing exactly the same thing.

"Good night, Kirsty," she murmured, yawning. "I can't wait to see you again soon. Eid Mubarak, and sweet dreams!"

The End

Now it's time for Kirsty and Rachel to help ...

Bea the Buddha Day Fairy

Read on for a sneak peek ...

... Rachel shut the door behind her and leaned against it, smiling.

"Happy Buddha Day," she said. "I've been thinking about Bea all morning."

"Me too," said Kirsty. "Wasn't our adventure with Elisha exciting?"

"Yes, and I was so surprised when you turned up at my window," said Rachel, laughing as she remembered. "Thank goodness we found the pelita lamp. I just hope that we can find Bea's magical candle too."

She started to unpack her bag. Kirsty always kept one of her drawers empty, ready for Rachel's visits.

"I hope Bea arrives soon," said Kirsty, longingly. "Buddhists all over the world are celebrating the birth of Buddha today. It's called the Vesak Festival. I can't bear to think of Jack Frost spoiling that, just so he can create his own festival."

Read Bea the Buddha Day Fairy to find out what adventures are in store for Kirsty and Rachel!

Calling all parents, carers and teachers!
The Rainbow Magic fairies are here to help
your child enter the magical world of reading.
Whatever reading stage they are at, there's
a Rainbow Magic book for everyone!
Here is Lydia the Reading Fairy's guide to
supporting your child's journey at all levels.

Starting Out

Our Rainbow Magic Beginner Readers are perfect for first-time readers who are just beginning to develop reading skills and confidence. Approved by teachers, they contain a full range of educational levelling, as well as lively full-colour illustrations.

Developing Readers

Rainbow Magic Early Readers contain longer stories and wider vocabulary for building stamina and growing confidence. These are adaptations of our most popular Rainbow Magic stories, specially developed for younger readers in conjunction with an Early Years reading consultant, with full-colour illustrations.

Going Solo

The Rainbow Magic chapter books – a mixture of series and one-off specials – contain accessible writing to encourage your child to venture into reading independently. These highly collectible and much-loved magical stories inspire a love of reading to last a lifetime.

www.orchardseriesbooks.co.uk

"Rainbow Magic got my daughter reading chapter books. Great sparkly covers, cute fairies and traditional stories full of magic that she found impossible to put down" - Mother of Edie (6 years)

"Florence LOVES the Rainbow Magic books. She really enjoys reading now"
- Mother of Florence (6 years)

Read along the Reading Rainbow!

Well done – you have completed the book!

This book was worth 1 star.

See how far you have climbed on the Reading Rainbow opposite.
The more books you read, the more stars you can colour in
and the closer you will be to becoming a Royal Fairy!

Do you want to print your own Reading Rainbow?

1) Go to the Rainbow Magic website

2) Download and print out the poster

3) Colour in a star for every book you finish
and climb the Reading Rainbow

4) For every step up the rainbow,
you can download your very own certificate

There's all this and lots more at
orchardseriesbooks.co.uk

You'll find activities, stories, a special newsletter
AND you can search for the fairy with your name!